BRENT LIBRARIES

Please return/renew this item
by the last date shown.
Books may also be renewed by
phone or online.
Tel: 0333 370 4700
On-line www.brent.gov.uk/libraryservice

BY FRANK LAMPARD

FRANKIE'S MAGIC FOOTBALL

SUMMER HOLIDAY SHOWDOWN

FRANK LAMPARD

LITTLE, BROWN BOOKS FOR YOUNG READERS
www.lbkids.co.uk

LITTLE, BROWN BOOKS FOR YOUNG READERS

First published in Great Britain in 2017 by Hodder and Stoughton

1 3 5 7 9 10 8 6 4 2

Copyright © Lamps On Productions, 2017

The moral rights of the author and illustrator have been asserted.

A CIP catalogue record for this book
is available from the British Library.

ISBN 978-1-51020-113-2

Printed and bound in Great Britain by
Clays Ltd, St Ives plc

The paper and board used in this book are made
from wood from responsible sources.

To my mum Pat, who encouraged me to do my homework in between kicking a ball all around the house, and is still with me every step of the way.

Welcome to a fantastic
Fantasy League – the greatest
football competition ever held
in this world or any other!

You'll need four on a team,
so choose carefully. This is a lot
more serious than a game in the
park. You'll never know who your
next opponents will be, or
where you'll face them.

So lace up your boots, players,
and good luck! The whistle's
about to blow!

The Ref

CHAPTER 1

Frankie lay on his stomach on his surfboard, watching the wave build behind him.

"Ready?" he shouted to Louise.

She was bobbing a few metres away. "Looks like a big one!" she called back.

As the surge of the wave rocked beneath him, Frankie started paddling hard with his arms. He felt

1

the water snatch him up and pull him fast towards the beach. Frankie gripped the board, then pushed himself up so both his feet were planted in the middle of the board. Slowly, he straightened his knees.

I'm doing it! he thought, as the surfboard cut through the water.

"Hey, Lou! Check this out!"

He looked across to where Louise, in her wetsuit, was expertly gliding on the crest of a wave, her knees slightly bent. She glanced over and gave him a thumbs-up.

And then it all went wrong. Frankie felt the board lurch forward, and suddenly his feet were

in the air. The water smashed into his side, and he was underwater. Foam and bubbles frothed around him, shooting up his nose. The water rolled his body, and he hit the seabed with a thump that knocked the wind from his stomach. He couldn't tell which way was up,

3

and thrashed his hands frantically. At last, gasping, he broke the surface and sucked in a breath. The remains of the wave carried him gently towards the beach, and the surfboard washed along at his side.

As the water cleared from his ears, Frankie heard his brother laughing.

"Wipe out!" said Kevin.

Frankie picked himself up in the shallows. Kevin was sitting on a towel on the beach, wearing sunglasses. Frankie's mum was lying on an inflatable lilo a few metres further up the beach with an open book resting on her chest.

"It's much harder than it looks,"

said Louise. She drifted in, still standing on her surfboard. "Are you okay Frankie?"

Frankie nodded. The pain in his side was fading. It wasn't the first knock he'd taken, and it wouldn't be the last. He grabbed the board. "Let's get out there again," he said.

But his mum woke up, sat up and looked at her watch. "Gosh is that the time?" she said. "We should get back to the hotel."

Frankie gazed out across the ocean. The water sparkled in the sun's rays, blue as far as the horizon. In the distance, boats dotted the vast expanse. They'd only been on holiday in Cornwall for a couple of days, staying in the Seatoller Hotel, and Frankie never wanted to leave.

"Where's Charlie?" asked Frankie's mum.

Kevin pointed along the beach. "He went with Max to explore the rock pools," he said. Frankie glanced across the crowded sand. Sunbathers lounged under parasols and kids were building sandcastles. Then Frankie saw Max and Charlie heading towards them. Max was wiggling his tail in excitement.Charlie was holding a bucket. He wore a wide-brimmed hat, and his body looked very white. Charlie burned really easily, so he had to wear layers and layers of sun cream.

"Look what we found," he said, as he came closer.

He set the bucket down and Frankie saw a large greenish crab in the bottom. It spread its pincers wide.

"Wow!" said Louise.

Frankie's mum let out a shriek. "I'm going back but don't be long."

Max peered over the edge of the bucket and whined.

"Max found it," said Charlie. "It pinched his nose!"

Frankie stroked his dog's neck. "Poor boy!" he said.

"We should cook the crab!" said Kevin.

"No!" they all replied at once.

"Let's put it back in the water," said Louise. Kevin agreed. She tipped the bucket carefully, and the crab scurried into the shallows. In a few seconds, it had vanished.

"I was watching you surfing, Lou," said Charlie. "You're really good!"

"Thanks," she replied.

"A lot better than Frankie," laughed Kevin.

Frankie scowled at his brother.

"Why don't you show us how it's done?" he said, offering his board.

Kevin went red. "I would, but I haven't got a wetsuit," he replied.

How convenient, thought Frankie.

"Come on, let's get back," said Louise.

They started to walk up the beach, and Kevin called after them. "Hey, wait for me!"

He was rolling up his towel, and putting on his flipflops.

"Just keep walking," said Frankie to his friends.

Their hotel was right on the cliff edge, at the top of a set of wooden

steps. The grand building dated from the nineteenth century — three storeys of weathered grey stone, with turrets at each corner. A leaflet in reception said it used to be a boarding school, years ago. In the afternoon sunlight, the windows glittered, but at night it looked sort of spooky. The floorboards creaked, and doors rattled in the wind.

Frankie was still smarting from Kevin's taunts as he and Louise peeled off their wetsuits and left their boards at the surf-rental shack. Sometimes he wished he didn't even *have* a brother.

As they went inside, they saw the rest of their parents in the lounge, drinking tea. "Hey, come and look at this," said Louise's dad. He was staring at a picture on the wall, near to the reception desk.

Frankie and the others went inside, followed by Kevin. The picture was a black and white photo – a school photo – showing rows of kids in uniforms with caps on their heads.

"Don't they all look miserable!" said Louise's dad.

Frankie scanned the faces. He was right – not a single person was smiling. The only teacher in the picture was a stocky man with his arms folded – he stared fiercely at the camera.

"It says it was taken in 1931," said Charlie, pointing to the date at the bottom of the picture.

"Then I'm glad I wasn't at school then," said Louise. "Mr Donald might be strict, but that guy looks *really* mean."

CHAPTER 2

Frankie headed upstairs with Max scampering at his heels. Louise and Charlie went to the room they were sharing. Frankie was supposed to be in with Kevin, but he'd been sleeping on the sofa in his friends' room so far. His things were all in Kevin's room though. When he went to get some clean clothes, Kevin was lying on his bed listening to music. As Frankie opened the wardrobe he saw straight away that the magic football was missing. His anger flared up.

"What have you done with it?" he snapped.

Kevin was always messing with his football. He knew all about what it was capable of – opening doorways to other worlds.

Kevin pulled out his earphones. "Done with what?"

"My football," Frankie muttered.

"I didn't touch your stupid football," his brother replied.

"Yeah, right?" said Frankie.

"I promise," said Kevin, holding up his hands.

Frankie's blood began to boil. *Why can't he just leave it alone?* "Well I left it in here," said Frankie. "And it didn't just walk away on its own."

Kevin just shrugged.

Frankie was about to say something else when he noticed the ball under his own bed. He frowned, and picked it up. It felt oddly warm, like it had been lying in the sunshine for hours.

"You hid it," he said to Kevin.

Kevin put his earpiece back in. "Fine, don't believe me," he said.

Holding the football, Frankie

grabbed his clean clothes and
headed to see Charlie and Louise.

They had fish and chips for dinner
at a nearby café. Kevin was quiet
throughout, and as they walked
back to hotel along the seafront, he
followed a short distance away. The
sun was going down, casting a trail of
red and gold across the sea.

Inside Frankie and his friends
went up to their bedroom. As
they walked in, Max was curled
in his basket underneath an old
grandfather clock. Frankie brushed
his teeth and settled onto the sofa,
pulling his blanket over him.

"Maybe tomorrow we should play with Kev," said Charlie.

"Why?" said Frankie. "He just ruins everything."

"He hasn't got any friends here," said Louise. "He might be nicer tomorrow."

"Maybe," said Frankie. He thought of his brother going to sleep on his own in the next room. *He'll be all right,* he told himself.

Frankie's limbs ached from the hours of surfing, and he felt his body sinking into the sofa cushions. When he closed his eyes, he could still feel the rocking of the sea. In no time at all, he was asleep.

He woke in the darkness with hair ticking his nose.

"Wake up," whispered a voice. "Frankie!"

Frankie rubbed his eyes and found himself face to face with Max, paws on the edge of the sofa.

"You're talking!" said Frankie.

"Yep," said Max.

"But you only talk when
the magic football takes us
somewhere," said Frankie.

"Something's up," said Max. "In
the wardrobe."

Louise and Charlie were stirring
in their beds.

The wardrobe door shifted a
little, like something was knocking
it from the inside.

Frankie flicked on the lamp
beside the sofa, squinting. Charlie
sat up, his red hair sticking out in a
frizzy mess. "What's going on?"

The door banged again, harder,
and everyone jumped.

"Rats?" said Max.

Frankie shook his head. "I think it must be the football. I put it in there to hide it from Kevin."

He climbed off the sofa and went to the wardrobe. He turned the door handle slowly. The door shot open before he could stop it and the football flew across the room, hitting the wall opposite.

"Woah!" said Louise. The ball wobbled for a second, then Frankie planted his foot on top of it. He could feel the ball straining beneath his sole.

"This is so weird," said Frankie. Normally he had to kick the ball in order to create a magical doorway —

it had never moved on its own before.

"Maybe we should see where it wants to go," said Charlie.

Frankie lifted his foot. The ball rolled around aimlessly.

Frankie felt a rush of guilt. *Maybe Kevin wasn't lying earlier. Maybe he didn't steal the ball.*

There'd be time to say sorry later. The ball came to rest up against the base of the grandfather clock. Frankie noticed it was half-past one.

Then something very odd happened. Before his eyes, the hands of the clock began to move.

23

Backwards!

"What's going on?" said Louise.

The hands moved faster and faster, until they were just a blur. Frankie blinked, as the room around him seemed to shift in and out of focus too. He felt dizzy, and weightless, like his body was drifting.

Then, suddenly, daylight came streaming through the window and everything was still again.

"Er ... what are you *wearing*?" said Louise.

Frankie looked down and saw he wasn't wearing his Chelsea pyjamas anymore. He had thick woollen shorts, a white shirt, and a buttoned up maroon jacket. His socks were pulled up to his knees and there were polished black shoes on his feet. Charlie was dressed the same.

"What are *you* wearing?" he said to Louise. She had on a white blouse and a maroon sleeveless dress. She winced. "Yuck! It's some sort of awful school uniform."

Frankie looked around the room, which had changed completely. There were thick curtains at the window, instead of blinds. Six single beds, all with the same brown bedclothes, lined the room. Beside

each was a narrow wardrobe and a small chest of drawers, with a single candle on top.

"It's a dormitory," he said.

A smile crept across Charlie's lips. "I think I know where we are," he said. "Remember that photo in the hotel lounge?"

"The school!" said Louise. "From the 1930s!"

Max sniffed at the football, which was still resting against the base of the clock. "Question is, why has the ball brought us here?" he said.

A creak made them all look up. Footsteps sounded through the wall, moving along the corridor outside. They paused, and a stern voice boomed, "Who's still up here?"

Frankie grabbed the football.

"Hide!" he whispered.

Max scurried under a bed, Louise ducked behind a wardrobe, and Frankie and Charlie squeezed into the spaces behind the curtains. He peered out through a gap as a man strode into the space. He had short powerful legs and a barrel chest. He wore a tight-fitting long-sleeve T-shirt and shorts. A huge moustache curled over his upper lip, and his beady eyes narrowed.

It's the teacher from the photo!

Frankie held his breath. The man peered around the room, then turned on his heel, closing the door behind him.

Thank goodness. We're safe ...

As the man's boots stomped away, Frankie sensed Charlie shifting uncomfortably at his side. He made out his friend's hand underneath his nose, a series of panicked breaths. Charlie was going to sneeze!

No ... Don't ...

"Aaaaachoo!"

CHAPTER 3

The footsteps paused then thundered back and the door was flung open.

"Who's there!" demanded the man.

Frankie crept out from his hiding place. Charlie, and Louise did the same but Frankie signalled to Max to stay put.

"Sorry," muttered Charlie.

The teacher glared at them. "What are you lot doing in here?" he said.

Frankie didn't know what to say, and it was Louise who spoke up. "We got lost," she said.

The teacher fixed her with his eyes. "*Lost?* LOST? It's lunchtime. Have you forgotten where the mess is?"

"What mess?" asked Charlie.

"That kind of cheek will land you on deck–scrubbing duty, boy." The teacher's eyes narrowed. "Who are you three anyway? I don't recognise your faces."

"We're ... um ..." Frankie stammered.

"Never mind," said the teacher. "You nippers all look the same to me." His glance fell on the football in Frankie's hands. He paused for a moment, frowning. "Where did you find that thing?"

"It's a football, sir," said Frankie.

The teacher snarled. "It's Captain Hardcastle to you, and I *know* it's a football. What's it's doing here?"

Before Frankie could do anything, the teacher grabbed the football from his hands. "We don't play namby-pamby games like that here. It's rugger, or nothing. Is that clear?"

"Yes, Captain," they all said.

"But Captain Hardcastle," said Frankie, "please can I have my ball back?"

Red spots appeared on the man's cheeks. "Of course not!" he said. "I'm confiscating it!"

Frankie gasped.

"Now get to the mess!" said the teacher, pointing towards the door.

Frankie glanced at the bed where Max was hiding. What choice did they have? He traipsed towards the door.

This is a disaster!

They emerged from the room into a corridor that looked just like the hotel, apart from the strange lamps

on the walls alongside portraits of
severe-looking men and women.
Frankie heard the sound of voices
and crockery clashing below.
Horrible food smells drifted up
his nostrils. They went down the
stairs, to where the hotel reception
had been. Only now it was a

wood-panelled entrance hall with a cabinet full of trophies and plaques. A girl ran past, giggling.

"Walk in the corridors!" snarled Captain Hardcastle from behind them, before stomping off with the football in hand.

They followed the girl, and soon reached a large room lined with tables and benches. It was the same room where breakfast was served in the hotel. There was a side hatch where kids queued with their plates. Frankie joined the back, wondering when he'd have an opportunity to go and fetch Max. He wasn't hungry at all, and when he saw the green slop being shovelled onto the plates, his stomach turned.

"What is *that*? muttered Louise.

The girl ahead of them turned. "Turnip mash and gristle stew. It tastes even worse that it looks."

"No chips?" said Charlie.

"You must be joking!" said the girl, then she frowned. "Why are you wearing those weird gloves?"

Frankie smiled, despite their circumstances. Charlie *never* took his goalie gloves off.

"His hands get cold," said Louise.

Once all three of them had had their plates filled, they went to an empty table.

Louise frowned at her plate, sniffed, and pushed it away. Charlie was already eating.

"It's not that bad," he said, chewing on some meat.

Frankie tasted some of the mashed turnip. "Even Max wouldn't eat this," he said.

"Why do you think we're here?" asked Louise. "Normally the football wants us to help someone."

Frankie glanced around the room. There were perhaps thirty kids at the tables, all wearing the same maroon uniforms. No one was speaking much. Then Frankie saw a skinny boy with sandy hair looking for somewhere to sit. On the first table he approached, the boys and girls shifted to fill the spare seat. He sighed and walked to the next. The same thing happened.

Why are they picking on him?

"There's a space here," called Frankie. The boy looked up, smiled faintly and began to walk over. He didn't see a leg extending into his path.

"Agh!" he cried, as he tripped over. The plate in his hand went flying, smashing on the floor. For a moment, there was silence, then laughter rang out through the room.

The boy stood up, his face flushed with rage. "Who did that?"

Another boy, at least a head taller than him, rose from his bench. "I did, little George. And what are you going to do about it? Set your brother on me?"

For a moment, the boy called George just glared. *There's nothing he can do,* thought Frankie. *Not if he's got any sense.* But George was breathing hard, like an angry bull. He lowered his head and charged straight into the bully. They landed across the table, scattering more plates and causing angry shouts.

Everyone was suddenly on their feet, roaring encouragement.

"This is horrible," said Louise. "We've got to stop it."

Just as Frankie was wondering how, a voice bellowed.

"Silence!"

Everyone hit their seats in a flash. Captain Hardcastle was standing in the doorway.

George and the boy he'd been fighting were still lying across a table-top, covered in food.

"Is someone going to tell me what's going on?" asked Captain Hardcastle. "Or will I have to keelhaul the lot of you?"

"It was George, Captain," said the larger boy. "He said the food was disgusting and threw it on the floor."

Captain Hardcastle strode further into the room, taking in the mess.

"Is that right, George?" he snapped.

"Yes, Captain," said George quietly.

"No!" cried Frankie. "That isn't what happened. *He* tripped George up!"

Captain Hardcastle's jawline hardened. "Mr Casey," he pointed at the bigger boy. "Come with me — you're on bailing duty."

Casey shot a cold glare at Frankie, then at George before following the grim-faced teacher. The other kids turned to watch him go. Frankie wondered what *bailing duty* could be.

Louise stood up. "Hey, George," she said. "You can have my food. I'm not hungry."

George shook his head, aghast "What have you done?"

"What do you mean?"

"You snitched on Casey. He'll never let me forget this!"

"But . . ."

George was already on his way out of the room.

A girl from the next table over leaned back. "George is like that with everyone. He's not been the same since his brother Alex ran away."

"Where did he go?" asked Louise.

"No one really knows," said the girl. "They were always arguing though. One day Alex was just gone. Left all his things behind."

"That's awful," said Charlie.

A bell went, ringing out through the school.

"Games!" said the girl. "We'd better go and get changed."

Frankie shrugged. "We haven't got any kit."

The girl made a sympathetic face. "Don't worry — the Captain will find you something to wear."

As they joined the procession leading from the dining hall, Frankie was deep in thought.

Maybe that's why the football brought us here. It wants us to find Alex so George can be happy again.

The problems seemed to be stacking up though; They'd lost the football, they'd made an enemy of George, and they didn't have the first clue where to start searching for George's brother.

Maybe this is one match we can't win . . .

CHAPTER 4

While everyone went to the changing rooms, Frankie held back and checked the dormitory again.

"Max?" he whispered.

His dog came out. "All clear?"

"For now," said Frankie, "but you should stay put. At least until we can get the football again."

"Do you want me to try and steal it back?"

"Too risky," said Frankie. "We don't want Captain Hardcastle confiscating you too."

"I'd like to see him try," said Max, baring his teeth.

Looking out of the window, Frankie saw Captain Hardcastle in the grounds below, checking a pocket watch as kids streamed past him. "I've got to go."

The changing rooms were in an outbuilding behind the school. As Frankie rushed to join the other students, he got a view of the seashore. The beach below was empty of holidaymakers.

From the grey sky and freezing air, Frankie guessed it was late autumn.

Some kids were already outside in their PE kit – grey flannel shorts and long-sleeve white T-shirts, plus shoes like plimsolls. George was among them, head low. But when Frankie went into the changing room, he saw a few kids were still getting dressed.

"You'd better hurry," said a boy.

"We haven't got any kit," said Charlie.

The boy smirked. "Look in the cesspit," he said.

"The cesspit?" said Louise.

The boy pointed to a chest against the wall.

Frankie went over. *It doesn't look like a cesspit.* But as he opened the lid, it smelled like one. Charlie covered his nose with his glove. "It stinks!"

"That's because none of it's ever been washed," said the boy.

"We can't wear that," said Louise.

The boy laughed. "Good luck telling Hardcastle that. He'll put you in the brig if you're not careful."

"What's *the brig*?" asked Frankie, as he fished for something that looked like his size.

"You get locked in the school cellar all day. Hardcastle just calls it that because he used to be at sea. It's completely dark down there. Freezing cold."

"That's illegal, surely," said Charlie.

The boy laughed. "Don't be daft.

Hardcastle makes the regs around here."

They got changed quickly into the sweaty old clothes.

"I think we need to help find George's brother," Frankie said to Charlie and Louise, under his breath.

"I don't think he wants our help," whispered Charlie. "Maybe the football brought us here by mistake."

"It *was* acting weird," added Louise.

A whistle blew. "We'd better go," said Frankie.

Outside, all the kids formed a

huddle in front of Mr Hardcastle. He was holding a rugby ball. *Cool*, thought Frankie. Mr Donald had taught them how to play touch rugby at school in the last term. It was great fun – plus, you could kick the ball sometimes, so it was a bit like football.

"Split into two teams," said the teacher pointing to opposite sides of the sports pitch.

Frankie couldn't see a goal, or any posts. "Er . . . what are the rules?" he asked.

"Simple," said a boy as they jogged to one end. "You have to get the ball to the far end of the pitch."

"Sounds fun," said Louise.

The boy looked at her like she was mad.

They lined up so they were facing the other team on the opposite side of the field. Captain Hardcastle placed the ball in the centre. He lifted his whistle to his lips.

Just at that moment, Casey came staggering up from the cliffs, carrying two buckets. Frankie noticed water was trickling from the bottom of each. He jogged to a barrel, and poured the contents from the buckets inside, then rested against the edge, breathing heavily.

"Back to it!" shouted Captain Hardcastle. "You can finish when the barrel is full."

With a weary glance, Casey began to run back towards the steps.

"The buckets have holes in!" said Louise.

"Exactly," said a girl on their side. "The quicker you run, the quicker you can fill the barrel."

So that's bailing duty, thought Frankie.

"That's like torture!" said Charlie.

"Welcome to Seatoller Hall," said the girl.

The shrill whistle carried across

the field. With a roar, both teams charged at each other like armies rushing into battle.

Casey's friend from the changing room reached the ball first, and snatched it up. He ran straight at George. Frankie expected him to pass or jink sideways at the last minute. Instead, he ran straight into George like a speeding truck. George flew through the air and landed on his back, where he lay groaning. *I think the rules here might be a bit different to the ones at our school*, thought Frankie. The massive kid was knocking others aside like skittles, but Charlie leapt in from one side, wrapped his gloves around the boy's hips, and brought him down. The ball rolled loose.

"We can do this!" called Frankie.

Louise flicked the ball with her toe. Its wobbling flight carried it over several heads, and Frankie swooped in to catch it. Straightaway, he saw several of his opponents closing in with bloodthirsty faces. Frankie backed away, looking for someone to pass to. He saw George, limping away from the action three quarters of the way up the field.

"Hey, George! Heads up!" he shouted.

He dropped the ball to his foot and booted it upfield, a perfectly weighted looping pass. George lifted his arms, ready to catch . . .

. . . and missed.

The ball hit his chest and bounced to the ground.

Laughing, another girl picked it up, then booted it away. Frankie ran to intercept, but an elbow to the ribs dropped him to the ground. All he saw for a few seconds were stamping feet and muddy legs, then he heard a cheer. He realised the other team had scored.

"One goal to nothing!" said Hardcastle. "Looks like some of you will be on half rations tonight!"

Frankie picked himself up and went across to his friends, who gathered back at the end of the pitch. As George came over, Frankie heard muttering among his teammates.

"Why did I have to be on George's team?"

"He couldn't even catch a cold!"

"What did he mean about half rations?" asked Charlie.

They lined up again, and Captain Hardcastle replaced the ball.

"The losing team forfeits half

their supper," said a boy. "That's why we have to win, so no more passing to butter fingers. Got it?"

Frankie glanced at George, who was staring at his own feet. *Poor guy. How's he ever going to improve if people are so mean to him?*

He sidled over. "Stick with me," he said.

George shook his head. "Just leave me alone," he muttered. "You're making things worse."

The next play was chaos. People running into each other, the ball flying loose. Just as it looked like one team might score, a last-ditch tackle or dropped ball turned the advantage to the other side. There were twisted ankles, bloody noses, dead-legs, eye-pokes, and even a dislocated finger. George, Frankie noticed, stayed well away from the action. Frankie understood why – *this game is bloodthirsty!*

CHAPTER 5

Each team managed two more points each, leaving the score at three–two.

"Last point!" called Captain Hardcastle.

"Right," said Frankie, back at his own end. Everyone was breathing hard, covered in mud. "We need to work together as a team. At the moment everyone's just running after the ball. We need our fastest runner to get the ball, then pass it back to the best thrower. Send the smaller kids through the gaps to the far end ready to catch, and the biggest kids need to form a line to stop the attackers."

"Who made you the boss?" someone grumbled.

"Do you want supper or not?" asked Louise.

That brought several nods, and they quickly arranged themselves into groups based on Frankie's instructions. When Captain Hardcastle blew the whistle, Louise sprinted to get the ball. The other player was quicker though, so Louise put in a sliding tackle to take it from him. She kicked it back to Charlie as their opponents rushed on. Frankie dodged and weaved through the mass of bodies, looking back over his shoulder to see Charlie cocking his arm like an American Football player. He launched the ball in a high arc. *Great throw.* Frankie continued his run, following the ball's path over his shoulder. He caught it right on the line, and placed it down.

"Touchdown!" he cried.

Everyone looked confused at that, but his team cheered.

"Three a piece," grumbled Captain Hardcastle. "Looks like you'll all be eating tonight."

Back in the changing room, Frankie and his friends got out of their smelly kit as fast as possible. They were the first to be ready, and as they trudged back towards the school ahead of everyone else, Frankie noticed a familiar face peeping from behind a bush.

He rushed over with Louise and Charlie.

"Max!" said Frankie. "Where've you been?"

"Sniffing around," said Max. "You're right about the football. It's in Hardcastle's study, but the door's locked."

"Great!" said Charlie.

"The window isn't though," said Max, his tail wagging.

"Clever boy," said Louise. "Show us."

Nobody had emerged from the

changing room yet, and there was no sign of Captain Hardcastle as they crept through the gardens to the side of the school. Max paused by a window and placed a paw on the glass. "There!"

Sure enough the magic football was sitting on the edge of a large desk in a room lined with sports equipment. The sash window was open, but only a few centimetres at the bottom.

"I'm going in," said Frankie.

"Are you sure?" asked Charlie. "If Hardcastle catches you, I think it'll be a lot worse than filling a barrel."

"We haven't got a choice," said Frankie. "George doesn't want our help, so I'm not getting stuck in the 1930s. The food's horrible, and they don't even play football."

He slipped his fingers beneath the edge and eased the window higher, squeaking a little. He clambered over the sill and into the room. A figure in the corner of the room made him jump, but as he gathered himself he realised it was a suit of armour. *What a weird thing for a teacher to have*, he thought. Frankie let out his breath. He was about to leave the room when something else caught his eye. On

one of the shelves between the books, was a golden ornament — a snake, finely engraved with jewels for eyes.

Looks like it's from Ancient Egypt, he thought. *It must be priceless!*

Beside it was a polished marble carving of a man in a toga who looked Roman, and next to it, a cowboy hat.

Maybe Hardcastle's some sort of collector . . .

"Frankie, hurry," murmured Louise.

Frankie grabbed the ball, dashed for the window and climbed out.

71

They drew down the sash as it was before.

"Okay, let's go home," said Louise. "I suppose we have to go back to the clock."

Frankie nodded. They crept back towards the entrance to the school, keeping a lookout for Captain Hardcastle, then dashed up the stairs. They found the dorm with the grandfather clock, and pressed inside, closing the door behind them.

"Hey!" said a voice. "Where'd you get that?"

Frankie jumped, and saw that George was sitting on one of the beds. From the streaks under his eyes, Frankie guessed he'd been crying. But his eyes were fixed on the magic football.

"It's just my football," said Frankie. He was wondering how they could get rid of George without being too mean.

But George didn't look like he was going anywhere. His face was pale, his features twisting with a mixture of shock and emotion, as he climbed off the bed. He didn't even seem to have noticed Max.

"No, *where* did you get it," he said.

Frankie glanced at his friends. Something weird was going on.

"Why are you so interested?" asked Charlie.

"Because," said George, his eyes narrowing, "that football belongs to *me*!"

Then he threw himself at Frankie like a madman.

CHAPTER 6

George bowled Frankie over
and they hit the ground hard.
Frankie tried to squirm out, but
George was stronger than he
looked. "Give it to me!" he yelled.

Eventually, Charlie and
Louise hoisted the smaller boy
off. His face was wild, and he
continued to struggle against
them.

"Calm down!" Frankie urged. "You're going to alert Mr Hardcastle ..."

Slowly, George ran out of steam, and hung limply between Charlie and Louise, his chest heaving.

"I need to have the magic football," he sobbed.

"Wait – *what*?" said Frankie. "How do you know it's magic?"

George glanced sorrowfully at Charlie and Louise. "You can let me go," he said.

Frankie's friends looked to Frankie, who nodded. George sat down on the edge of a bed, with his shoulders slumped.

"You said the football belonged to you," said Charlie. "How is that possible?"

"My brother and I found the ball at the back of the sports cupboard when we were sneaking around. And then we learned of its powers. We used to go on adventures together, until ..." He trailed off.

"Until what?" asked Louise gently.

"Alex was older than me," said George. "We used to argue a lot. I suppose we both had hot tempers. One time, we disagreed about using the football. I said we should take a break, he didn't want to. Then, one day about a month ago, he disappeared."

Frankie let the story sink in. He'd never known that anyone had owned the football before he'd won it at a fair. George looked close to tears again.

"So your brother didn't run away from school," said Frankie.

George shook his head. "No. But I could hardly tell everyone he'd gone through a magical doorway."

Frankie knew how he felt. He'd lost count of the number of times the football had landed them in awkward spots.

"I think the magic football

brought us here to help you," he said. "If you'll let us?"

"Help *me*?" said George, his face brightening. "Why would you?"

"Because it's the right thing to do," said Louise. "Have you any idea where Alex might be?"

"Yes!" George hopped off the bed, and went to his chest of drawers. He pulled one out completely, then flipped it over on the bed, spilling the clothes. Taped to the underside was a piece of parchment paper, discoloured with age. There were markings on it.

"A map!" said Charlie. "It looks really old."

They crowded closer. Frankie saw
it was an island, and there was an X
marked on the eastern side

"It's a treasure map," said
George. "We won it from a bunch
of real pirates on one of our
adventures."

Frankie smiled. They'd faced

80

some pirates too once – and had almost been fed to the sharks!

"I think Alex went looking for the treasure," said George. "But he must have failed, because he never came back. Nor did the ball, until now."

"Someone's coming!" said Max.

Frankie heard it too. Footsteps creaking along the hallway outside.

"Hardcastle!" said George. He quickly stuffed the map into the drawer and replaced it. Frankie shoved the magic football under a pillow. Then they all stood stock still, holding their breath. The footsteps stopped outside the room ...

. . . then continued along the corridor.

Frankie and the others waited for a few minutes, then Frankie said, "Let's find Alex."

George nodded, and fished out the map. Then he held out a hand for the football. "May I?"

Frankie handed it over. With the map on the floor, George held the football over the top. "Ready?" he said.

Frankie and his friends gathered around.

George dropped the football, but when it hit the map, it fell straight through, vanishing. The floorboards under their feet went soft like jelly, then all around the walls dissolved. Frankie felt a warm breeze against his skin, and squinted against a bright light.

When he could see again, the dormitory had vanished, and he was standing in the mouth of a cave, above a stretch of white sand dotted with palm trees, under a cloudless blue sky. Waves sloshed against the shore. Frankie turned on the spot, hand up to shield his eyes. All he saw was clear ocean stretching to the horizon. Behind them, in the cave, the ball sat on the ground in front of a blurred patch of air in the rough shape of a circle.

The doorway home.

"Alex!" called George. "Alex?"

There was no answer.

"Let's split up and search for him," said Louise.

Charlie leant down to pick up the ball. "No, leave it there," said Frankie. "If that doorway closes, we might get stuck here."

They walked down the beach, fanning out and calling Alex's name. The only answer was the rustle of the wind through the palm leaves and the crashing of the waves.

"Hey, check this out!" called

Max. He was nosing at the sand, and as Frankie approached, he saw makings.

"Footprints!" he called. The others crowded nearer.

"Let's follow them," said Charlie.

And so they did. The track led along the beach, round a small patch of rocks. On the other side, Frankie stopped. He frowned.

"What on earth..." said George.

The sand ahead was pockmarked with holes – hundreds of them – each about a metre apart. Beside each was a mound of sand.

"You think some sort of animal made them?" asked Louise.

"What, a sand mole?" asked Max.

"They're too regular," said Frankie. He edged closer to one. It was a metre deep, and about a metre wide.

Then, from one of the holes further along the beach, a head emerged, wearing a dirty maroon school cap. He squinted, looking at Frankie and his friends. "Who are you?" he asked, then his gaze fell on George.

"Alex?" gasped George.

The other boy climbed out of the hole with a shovel in his hands. His skin was deeply tanned, and he had strong wiry arms. His long shorts

were torn and salt-stained. He tossed the shovel aside.

"George," he replied.

George smiled and ran towards his brother, hopping over the holes in the sand.

Frankie shared a smile with his friends. "Well, that wasn't too hard."

But Alex just stood where he was, and as George tried to throw his arms around him, Alex shoved him in the chest. His face was twisted with anger. With a roar, he threw himself on top of his brother.

CHAPTER 7

The brothers rolled in the sand, punching and kicking each other.

What's going on? Frankie asked himself.

"Stop them!" shouted Charlie.

Frankie and his friends ran forwards, and they managed to pull the two fighting brothers apart.

"What's the matter with you?"

said George, aghast. He climbed to his feet, his collar torn.

"Don't play the fool," snapped Alex, while Louise was holding him back. "You left me here!"

"No, I didn't!" shouted George. "*You* stole the football and sneaked off here."

"You were too chicken to come," said Alex. "But then you followed me anyway and *abandoned* me."

"That's ridic—"

"Okay, stop!" said Frankie, standing between them.

The brothers fell silent, eyeballing one another. George

didn't *look* like the sort of person who'd abandon his brother.

"We need to get to the bottom of this," said Louise. "Alex, what exactly happened?"

"Like I said, George didn't have the stomach to come to the island with me. He always was a bit of a wimp." George started to protest, but Frankie held up a hand. "So I came myself," said Alex. "I brought a shovel to find the treasure. Anyway, I dug for ages with no luck. When I decided to head back, the football had gone. I was stuck here." He pointed to his brother. "*He* was the only one who knew about it. He must have come through the portal as well, nicked the football and gone home."

"That's not true!" said George. "I was worried about you. You just vanished!"

"Right," said Max. "Maybe the ball just rolled off into the sea. Maybe a turtle stole it, or a seabird."

"Not likely," scoffed Alex.

It does seem a long shot, thought Frankie. He wasn't sure why, but something was troubling him, niggling away at his brain.

"Well it *wasn't* me," said George, folding his arms.

"The point is, we're here now," said Louise, "and we can get you home."

Alex sniffed. "You know, I never thought I'd say it, but I miss Seatoller Hall. Even the food." He gestured towards the sand a short distance away, where dozens of brown objects littered the ground.

"I've lived on coconuts and dried seaweed for a month!"

"I like coconuts!" said Charlie.

Alex rolled his eyes. "So did I. At first!"

"And you still haven't found the treasure?" asked Frankie.

"No," said Alex. He nodded out to sea. "The sun comes up over there, so that's east. I've dug all these holes but not found a thing. Maybe the map was wrong. I don't care anymore."

"Told you it was too dangerous," muttered George.

Fire leapt into Alex's eyes again, but it quickly died. "So anyway, how did you all get here, if you didn't have the ball all along?"

"We've got the ball now," said Frankie. He introduced the others. "It brought us to your school." He explained about the holiday, and how the school was a hotel now.

"That's incredible," said Alex. "Who'd want to stay at Seatoller Hall though?"

"It's nicer in our time," said Louise.

They trudged up the beach. "So let me get this straight," said Alex. "The ball somehow disappeared from the cave and ended up in the future?"

It is pretty amazing, thought Frankie. But he was still feeling uneasy.

"I suppose we'll never now exactly how," said Louise, "but I have a feeling it's had lots of owners over the years."

They were almost back at the cave where the ball had first brought them onto the island when Frankie realised what it was that troubled him. The objects in Captain Hardcastle's study ... from Ancient Egypt, from Rome, from the Wild West and from the Middle Ages. They were all places Frankie and his friends had visited using the magic football.

"Guys," he said. "I've got an idea who did steal the magic football."

"I thought we'd decided it was a seagull," said Alex.

"No," said Frankie. *Why didn't I see it before?* "I think it was . . . "

"*Hardcastle!*" George exclaimed.

Frankie looked up, standing in the cave mouth was the teacher from Seatoller Hall, with a wicked grin on his face. He had the magic football under one arm and a sack in the other. Max growled.

"And where do you think you lot are going?" he asked.

"You stole the ball!" said Alex.

"I commandeered it," said their teacher with a shrug.

"You left me here!"

"I was going to come back eventually," said Captain Hardcastle, "but then I managed to lose the ball on one of my voyages."

Frankie narrowed his eyes. "I saw the things in your study – you just use the football to steal things."

Captain Hardcastle's eyes flashed with anger, then he tossed the sack in front of them. "Maybe you're right. Open it."

Frankie looked inside, and tipped out four shovels.

"Get digging," said Captain Hardcastle.

"Are you kidding?" said George. "We've got to get back to school."

"Oh, you can go back," said Captain Hardcastle, "but not until you find this buried treasure."

Frankie took a step forward, wondering if he could rush at Hardcastle and somehow tackle him.

Louise pulled him back. "Don't!" she said.

"Listen to your friend," said

the teacher. "If you try any funny business, I'll make a doorway home and you'll all be trapped here forever. I wonder who you'd eat first. The dog perhaps?"

"I'd love to sink my teeth into you!" said Max.

Captain Hardcastle looked taken aback. "A talking dog? I suppose I shouldn't be surprised. You look a bit stringy, I must say."

Max looked ready to pounce. "Leave it, boy," said Frankie. *How has it come to this? We were only trying to help George and now we're in danger of being marooned on a desert island.*

He stooped down and picked up a shovel, then turned despairingly to his friends.

"What choice do we have?" he asked.

CHAPTER 8

"I'll wait right here," said Captain
Hardcastle. "Whistle when you find
something."

Frankie passed shovels to the
others. George and Alex were
glaring at their teacher.

"Come on," said Frankie. "We'd
better start digging."

"What a crook!" said Alex, as

they walked together back down the beach.

"He must have heard you talking about it!" said George. "You never were very careful."

"Oh, so it's *my* fault, is it?"

"Guys, enough!" said Louise. "Do you ever stop arguing?"

They reached the holes again. Alex had dug them in neat rows up and down the beach. He sank his spade into a bare patch of sand. "I hope the map's right," he said. "Otherwise we could be here a *loooong* time."

The others all took up spots at regular intervals.

They began to dig, the kids with shovels, and Max with his paws.

Frankie heaved spadeful after spadeful over his shoulder. *Dig, scoop, throw.* It was easy going at first, where the sand was soft, but soon the grains became moister, and the sand was heavier. He had to climb down to dig deeper and his back began to ache. Sweat poured over his forehead.

Dig, scoop, throw.

"What a pickle!" said George.

"I never liked Hardcastle," said Alex, "but even I didn't think he was capable of this."

Frankie finished his first hole,

climbed out, then headed along the row to begin another. Louise and Charlie were almost finished with theirs.

Dig, scoop, throw.

Frankie set to work again, his mind searching for answers. *How can we get out of this mess?*

His hands slipped on the shovel handle and pain burned through his palms. Looking down, he saw blisters were already forming. He heard grunts coming from the others.

As each of them finished a hole, they moved on to the next. Frankie watched the sun move slowly overhead. For a while, he kept count of the holes he'd dug, but then he started to wonder – *what's the point?*

The blisters under his fingers burst, then new ones began to form. As he straightened, he heard his back crick. His arms felt like lead.

"Why didn't you check if you were being followed?" grumbled Alex.

"Why didn't *you* check if *you* were being followed?" said George.

Couldn't they stop squabbling?

Dig, scoop, throw.

"None of this would have happened if you'd just come with me," said Alex.

Frankie expected to hear George snap back, but he didn't.

Instead, there was a groan and a thud.

"George?" said Alex.

No answer.

Frankie peered out of his hole towards George's, but he couldn't see him. He climbed out, and the others did the same. George had collapsed in his hole, slumped against the side with his eyes closed. His skin looked waxy and pale.

"George!" cried Alex. He leapt into the hole as well, cradling his brother. "Oh, George, wake up! I didn't mean it!"

"Get him into the shade," said Louise. "It's probably just sunstroke."

Together, they manhandled George from the hole. His eyelids were already flickering as they carried him under a palm tree where it was slightly cooler.

"What's going on over there?" called Captain Hardcastle. Frankie noticed he'd moved closer, peering in their direction. "Why've you stopped digging?"

"George needs water!" shouted Alex.

"Well, I haven't got any," said Captain Hardcastle. "You youngsters have no stamina."

"That man's a monster," said Louise. She was fanning George's face with a fallen palm leaf. Alex looked terrified, his eyes full of concern.

"If something happens to him, I'll never forgive myself."

"He'll be okay," said Louise. "But he needs fluids."

"We're surrounded by fluids," said Max, tongue lolling.

"Not salt water!" said Louise. "That'll only make him more ill."

"What about coconut water?" said Alex.

"Perfect," said Louise.

Alex ran across the beach, and picked up one of the coconuts. He lay it on its side, took careful aim with the edge of his shovel, and gave it a hard whack. The coconut shell cracked open. Picking it up

carefully, Alex came back and held the coconut to his brother's parched lips. The liquid inside was slightly milky, and most of it splashed over George's chin. He began to cough and splutter, but colour returned to his cheeks.

"George, are you all right?" asked Alex.

George gazed at his brother in confusion. "I think so."

"Right, back to it!" bellowed Hardcastle.

"George, you have to rest," said Alex.

George nodded, sitting against the tree. The others, Frankie included, took a few sips from the coconut. It tasted sweet and refreshing. Then they went back to work in their holes. As soon as Frankie sank his spade again, he hit something hard.

His heart almost stopped. Falling to his knees, he scooped sand with his hands, finding the edges of the buried object. It was wooden, with patches of leather — a chest!

"I've found it!" he cried. "I've found the treasure."

CHAPTER 9

In seconds, all the others, and George, were at the edges of the hole. Frankie continued to empty out the sand, until he found a metal clasp on one side.

"Open it," said Alex, in a whisper.

Frankie tried to prise the clasp open. At first it didn't budge, but he managed to work it loose. He lifted the lid.

"Golly!" said George.

The trunk was full of gold and silver plates, cups and coins, and enormous jewels set into necklaces and rings, bracelets and chains.

"This will be worth a fortune," said Charlie.

"And it will all be mine," said Captain Hardcastle. He stood

behind them, peering over. The light of the gold reflected in his eyes, making them glitter. He tossed them the sack in which he'd brought the shovels. "Start loading it up."

Frankie glanced back to the cave mouth. He thought he might be able to out-sprint the Captain back to the portal. But he knew the others probably couldn't, especially not George. *We've got no choice but to do what he says.*

Hardcastle seemed to read his mind, because he headed back towards the magical doorway. "I'll be waiting," he said. "Once it's all in the sack, you'll be free to go."

Yeah, right! thought Frankie.

He watched the teacher walk away, but already a plan was forming in his head.

"Max," he said. "I've got an idea."

Max cocked his head. "Something tells me I'm not going to like this."

Frankie arched his eyebrows. "No, probably not, but it might be our only chance of escaping this place."

A short while later, Frankie and Louise dragged the bulging sack across the sand, followed by Charlie and the two brothers. Captain Hardcastle, waiting beside the doorway, rubbed his hands together gleefully.

"Stop there," he barked, when they were a few metres away. They did as he said. "Now back off," he said.

Frankie remained where he was. "How do we know we can trust you?"

Captain Hardcastle gave them a smile that made Frankie think of a wolf eyeing up a rabbit. "I could just leave you here," he said. "If I come back in a few months, the treasure will still be here, but you lot will be skeletons!"

"He's got a point," said Louise.

They stepped back a few paces. Hardcastle approached the sack. Frankie watched him closely.

"You're up to something," said the teacher. "I bet you've just filled this with sand and coconut shells, haven't you?"

He loosened the top of the sack, then looked inside. Frankie waited, expecting the worst, but Captain Hardcastle reached inside and pulled out a golden twin candlestick. He whistled. "That will look *very* nice on my desk."

"You won't get away with this," sneered Alex.

"I already have," said Hardcastle.

He dragged the sack back towards the doorway. "See you later, landlubbers!"

He was about to jump through when the sack in his grasp wriggled. The teacher looked down at the same moment as Max's snout emerged. With a growl, the little dog fastened his teeth around Hardcastle's wrist. He screamed, but Max held on.

"Get this mutt off me!" he roared, shaking his arm up and down.

The kids rushed past him, jumping one by one through the portal, but Frankie remained.

"Run!" growled Max, still with a mouthful of Captain Hardcastle's sleeve.

I can't leave him!

Frankie lowered his shoulder and ran at the teacher, like he was tackling in rugby. He drove right into Hardcastle's side, with all the power he could muster. They toppled together, teacher, dog and boy, into the mouth of the cave.

Oooomph!

Frankie hit the ground, but it wasn't sand beneath him. He looked up to see the dormitory at Seatoller Hall. Captain Hardcastle lay beside him, and Max was barking wildly with a piece of torn sleeve in his jaws. The others looked down in astonishment.

Hardcastle sprang up first, face red with fury. "I'll have you all keelhauled for this!" He looked around at his feet. "Hey, where's my treasure?"

Frankie realised the sack was still on the island. The portal was still open, a blurred patch on the floor, with the ball and map resting just at the edge. But it was already beginning to shrink.

"No!" cried Captain Hardcastle. He jumped towards the portal, disappearing through the floor.

But as he did, the magical doorway portal vanished to nothing. Frankie watched the floorboards reform, and the ball rolled off the map.

"What does that mean?" asked Charlie.

"We can't just leave him there," said Frankie. He moved the ball back onto the map, and waited, but no portal opened.

"It looks like the football has made the decision for us," said Louise.

"Good riddance, Captain!" said George. "Let's see how you cope living on coconuts."

"At least he had his treasure,"

said Louise. "Not that there's anything to spend it on."

Alex jumped up onto one of the beds. "This'll make a nice change after sleeping on the sand."

"Hey, that's *my* bed!" said George.

"No, it's not," said Alex. "You're by the window until December."

"*It is* December. You've been gone a month, remember?"

"Yeah, but I haven't *been* here."

"So?"

"Arm wrestle for it!"

Louise glanced at Frankie and mouthed, "*Brothers!*"

CHAPTER 10

As George and Alex argued, the magic football was vibrating on the ground, then it rolled past Frankie, coming to rest up alongside the grandfather clock. At once, the hands began to move faster, swinging through the minutes as if they were seconds.

"I think it might be time for us to go home," said Frankie.

"We could come with you," said George, eyes widening. "It's got to be better than being at school — even if Hardcastle has gone!" He glanced at his brother Alex. "Fancy another adventure?"

Alex looked uncertain. "You know what. I think I've had enough adventures for now. How about we just stay here?"

"Chicken," said George.

"Who are you calling chicken?" said Alex, jumping down from the bed. "You're the one who ..." He stopped, then grinned. Both brothers started laughing.

The clock's hands were blurring.

"We owe you our gratitude," said George. "Thank you!" he said.

"High-five," said Frankie, holding up a palm.

George frowned. "What's a *high-five*?"

"Never mind," said Frankie. He shook George's hand instead, then Alex's.

The clock began to chime as the hands spun round. Frankie moved towards it with the others at his side. The floor felt like it was tipping slightly, and the room began to dim, until all he could really see was the clock-face, spinning and spinning. Then he felt

a rush of a wind, whipping through his clothes.

Everything went dark.

"Wake up, sweetie!"

Frankie squinted into the light, and his mum's face came into focus above him. He was lying on the sofa bed. The grandfather clock was chiming softly beside him.

"You're going to miss breakfast," said his mum. She was already dressed.

Frankie sat up. Louise and Charlie were stirring as well. Max stretched in his basket.

"What time is it?" asked Frankie.

"Nine o'clock," his mum said. "Not like you to sleep in, Frankie."

Frankie was confused. He didn't remember coming back from the boarding school. Had it all been a dream? He climbed out of bed and went to the wardrobe. The magic football was resting on a shelf.

"You know, Frankie," said his mum, "it's a bit mean not to share a room with your brother. He'll be all on his own in there."

Frankie, still confused, replied, "I think he prefers that."

His mum sighed. "It might seem that way sometimes, but Kevin's your brother. Give him a chance."

"All right," mumbled Frankie.

As his mum left the room, Frankie turned to Charlie and Louise. "Did I just dream it, or did we—?"

"Yes!" they both replied.

"But I just woke up in bed!" said Louise.

"Me too," said Charlie.

Max shook himself, and sand scattered from his fur.

Definitely not a dream.

They got dressed quickly and headed downstairs. On the way past the hotel reception, Louise stopped by the old school photograph. "Hey, check it out," she said.

Frankie and Charlie went to her side, peering at the black and white image.

"It's changed!" said Charlie. "Look, Hardcastle's gone."

Frankie scanned the rows, and saw his friend was right. The fierce teacher was nowhere to be seen. Then his eyes fell on two grinning faces in the middle row. George and Alex, side by side.

"Maybe they learned to get along after all," said Frankie.

The smell of bacon and sausages reached his nose. "Come on – I'm famished!"

The dining room was emptying

out, and Charlie went straight to their normal table. Frankie was about to sit down too when he noticed his brother, sitting alone in the far corner. Kevin was reading a book, moving some scrambled eggs around his plate. He even looked a bit sad.

As Frankie watched, he thought about what his mum had said upstairs, and about George and Alex.

"Hey, I'll catch up with you guys later," he said to Charlie and Louise.

He walked across the dining room to Kevin's table, and pulled

out a chair. His brother looked
up sharply. "What do you want,
Frankenstein?"

"Just wondered if I could sit
here?"

"Why?" said Kevin.

Frankie shrugged and turned

136

away. "Fine. If you want to be on your own . . ."

"No, wait," said Kevin. "I'm sorry."

Frankie paused, then sat down. "What are you going to do today?"

"Dunno," said Kevin. "I might just stay at the hotel."

"Fancy playing beach cricket?" asked Frankie. "We met some kids yesterday who wanted a game."

"You want me to play with you guys?" said Kevin, as if he couldn't believe it.

"Sure," said Frankie. "As long as you don't hog the bat."

Kevin grinned. "Worried I'll show you up?"

Frankie smiled back. "Something like that," he said.

Outside, through the windows, the sun sparkled on the calm water. It looked like it was going to be a fantastic day.

ACKNOWLEDGEMENTS

Many thanks to everyone at Hachette Children's Group; Neil Blair, Zoe King, Daniel Teweles and all at The Blair Partnership; Kieron Ward for bringing my characters to life; special thanks to Michael Ford for all his wisdom and patience; and to Steve Kutner for being a great friend and for all his help and guidance, not just with the book but with everything.

Frankie and his friends have
been on so many adventures,
taking them all over the world!

Turn the page for an extract
from another one of Frank
Lampard's books: *Frankie and
the World Cup Carnival* ...

The World Cup Tournament is taking place in Brazil, and Frankie and his friends are watching every game they can on the TV. So when one of their favourite players – Ricardo – starts talking to them from behind the TV screen, they know they're about to go on an adventure! At this point in the story, Frankie and his friends have just travelled through a portal created by the magic football ...

The world went dark for a few seconds, then Frankie realised he could hear distant chanting. He could smell sweat and grass and leather.

He opened his eyes and found himself in a changing room, with shirts hanging on pegs, and other kit strewn on benches. His friends were all around him, their faces puzzled. Max gave himself a shake.

"Nice of you to join me," said a voice.

They all span round and saw Ricardo standing behind them wearing a tracksuit and holding the magic football. Frankie couldn't believe he was there in the flesh.

"Hi," was all he managed to say.

Ricardo looked Frankie up and down, then glanced at the others. "You look very young to have the football," he said.

"I won it at a fair," said Frankie, feeling a bit stupid.

"We've won every game we've played so far," said Louise, lifting her chin proudly.

"Best goal–keeping record in the fantasy league," added Charlie.

Max wagged his tail. "Toughest defence on four legs too," he barked.

Frankie grinned — it was nice to have a *talking* dog again.

Kevin, for once, didn't say anything at all. He hadn't been a part of their team, until today.

"Well, this challenge will be a lot tougher than anything you've faced before," said the Brazilian.

Frankie stepped forward. "We're ready. You said the World Cup was in trouble?"

Ricardo sagged on to a bench, placing the ball beside him. He nodded gravely. "Three items have been stolen," he said. "Without them, the Final will not happen."

"What are they?" asked Charlie.

Ricardo counted them off on his fingers. "The head referee's whistle, the ball that will kick-off the Final and, last of all, the trophy itself."

"Can't you call the police?" asked Kevin.

The Brazilian laughed emptily. "The police can't help with this," he said. "A magical problem requires a magical solution."

"So can't they just find another ball and another whistle?" said Kevin.

Ricardo shook his head. "You

don't understand. These objects aren't just *things.* They have magical properties. The ball gives the players skills, the whistle ensures fair play, and the trophy — that's the most important of the three — is the spirit of football itself, the object which drives teams to win."

Kevin scoffed. "I don't believe it," he said.

Frankie glared at his brother, but Ricardo simply walked to the door. "Follow me, and I'll show you," he said.

As soon as he opened the door, Frankie heard the noise of the roaring crowd. "We're in a stadium, aren't we?"

Ricardo led them down a tunnel, and the noise grew louder all the time. At the end, he pointed. "Not just any stadium."

Frankie rocked back on his heels as he saw the white shirts of the players on the pitch and the huge stands on every side. "It's England and Argentina," he said. "We're in Brazil!"

FRANKIE'S MAGIC FOOTBALL WEBSITE

Have you had a chance to check out **frankiesmagicfootball.co.uk** yet?

Get involved in **competitions**, find out **news** and **updates** about the series, play **games** and watch **videos** featuring the author, **Frank Lampard!**

Visit the site to join **Frankie's FC** today!